Going Places

ON A BIKE

By Robert M. Hamilton

Gareth Stevens
Publishing

Please visit our website, www.garethstevens.com. For a free color catalog of all our high-quality books, call toll free 1-800-542-2595 or fax 1-877-542-2596.

Library of Congress Cataloging-in-Publication Data

Hamilton, Robert M., 1987-
On a bike / Robert M. Hamilton.
   p. cm. — (Going places)
Includes index.
ISBN 978-1-4339-6267-7 (pbk.)
ISBN 978-1-4339-6268-4 (6-pack)
ISBN 978-1-4339-6265-3 (lib. bdg.)
1. Bicycles—Juvenile literature. 2. Cycling—Juvenile literature. I. Title.
TL412.H36 2012
388.3′472—dc23

                                        2011030080

First Edition

Published in 2012 by
Gareth Stevens Publishing
111 East 14th Street, Suite 349
New York, NY 10003

Copyright © 2012 Gareth Stevens Publishing

Editor: Katie Kawa
Designer: Andrea Davison-Bartolotta

Photo credits: Cover, pp. 1, 5, 9, 13, 15, 17, 19, 23, 24 (brake, pedal) Shutterstock.com; pp. 7, 24 (wheels) Hemera/Thinkstock; p. 11 jupiterimages/Brand X Pictures/Thinkstock; p. 21 NizamD/Shutterstock.com.

Printed in the United States of America

CPSIA compliance information: Batch #CW12GS: For further information contact Gareth Stevens, New York, New York at 1-800-542-2595.

Contents

People love to ride bikes!

Bikes move on
two wheels.

Some bikes have
two small wheels, too.

These wheels help kids learn to ride.

A bike has two pedals.

A person's feet push
the pedals. This is
how a bike moves.

A bike has a brake.
This makes it stop.

People ride bikes
to stay healthy.
It is a good exercise.

A road bike is
a fast bike.
It is used for racing.

Some bikes do tricks!
These are called
BMX bikes.

Words to Know

brake

pedals

wheels

Index